John Taylor Terry

**Rev. Edward Taylor, 1642-1729**

John Taylor Terry

**Rev. Edward Taylor, 1642-1729**

ISBN/EAN: 9783337009052

Printed in Europe, USA, Canada, Australia, Japan

Cover: Foto ©Raphael Reischuk / pixelio.de

More available books at **www.hansebooks.com**

# REV. EDWARD TAYLOR

1642-1729

NEW-YORK
PRIVATELY PRINTED
1892

It is always a pleasure to look back to a notable and virtuous ancestry, and I have felt it a duty to have this little volume printed for the benefit of the descendants of Rev. Edward Taylor and Ruth Wyllys his wife, of Governor John Haynes and Mabel Harlakenden, of Governor Wyllys and his descendants, of Governor William Bradford of the Mayflower, and, through them, especially of the descendants of Rev. John Taylor and Elizabeth Terry his wife. I am led to do this from the fact that I have possession of many of the papers of the late Hon. Henry Wyllys Taylor, LL. D., of Canandaigua, New-York, who died there about six years ago, at the age of ninety-three years. Judge Taylor spent much time during his long life in making genealogical researches, and it has seemed to me proper that the facts herein stated should be made known to the parties interested. A part has been published in the "New-York Evangelist." I have added a written sketch by Miss Emma C. Nason, which was published in a series of articles in the "Advocate and Guardian" in 1880 and 1881. As it would be difficult to correct the error which will be apparent to the reader, in the first part of Miss Nason's article, I have inserted it as it was printed, with the subsequent correction.

JOHN TAYLOR TERRY.

New-York, April, 1892.

# REV. EDWARD TAYLOR.

R EV. EDWARD TAYLOR was born at Sketchley, near Coventry, Leicestershire, England, in 1642. His parents educated him for the ministry among the Dissenters, but their sufferings became very severe after 1662. The ejection of two thousand dissenting clergymen and the persecution which followed induced him to a voluntary exile. He remained some years after the passing of the Act of Uniformity, and sailed from England in 1668. He had declined to take the oath required of all Dissenters after the restoration of Charles II. At this distance of time it is difficult to obtain information respecting his family connections in England, although, as he spent four years at Cambridge University, it may be supposed that they were of a superior class. An acrostic letter which he wrote contained the names of two brothers and one sister, James, Samuel, and Alice.

From the date of his sailing from England till he reached this country, and for some time thereafter, he kept a diary with daily insertions, from which I make some extracts.

" A. D. 1668 April 26, being Lord's day, I came for sea taking boat at Execution Dock, Wapping, and a smooth tide, a gentle gale of wind and a prosperous fare to Gravesend," etc. The journal continues until, as recorded : "Lord's day May 3. I had a sad forenoon but toward evening the Shipmaster sent for me to go to prayer with them." And again, "Lord's day May 24. The wind in the morning was very low, yet a right northeast wind, etc., afterwards it was higher. I then being *put to exercise* spake from John 3rd Ch., 3rd v." "Lord's day June 14th. I exercised from Isaiah 3rd 11th." "Lord's day June 21st. I applied the doctrine I delivered the previous Lord's day." "Saturday, July 4th. . . . After the day clearing up we saw land on both hands, Plymouth on the left and Salem on the right. About five o'clock we saw the Islands in our passage up to Boston." "Lord's day July 5th. About three o'clock we came ashore."

He brought letters to Increase Mather, with whom he lodged two nights; also to "Mr. Mayo, minister of God's word to his people who meet in the new meeting house," and to John Hull the Mint Master, who invited him to his house till he was settled in college, and also invited him to bring his chest to his warehouse. "This gentleman would not be said Nay, therefore I was with him and received much kindness from him. I continued with him, until I settled at Cambridge."

"July 14th I went to Cambridge to speak with the President [Chauncey]." "July 23rd. Being settled in College pupil under Mr. Thomas Graves, Senior Fellow, I continued there three years and a quarter," etc. Again, "Mr. Graves not having his name for naught, lost the love of the Undergraduates by his too great austerity, whereupon they used to strike a nail above the hall door catch while we were reciting to him in the Hall at which disorder I was troubled, etc. When he went to read to us 'Natural Physic' he would read to us out of Maguirus which was reputed none of the best, and which had not been read by the other classes in the College and so we did refuse to read it, and I also (although since I read it am sorry I opposed it) insomuch that he seeing he could not prevail with me to read it through . . . gave me the unworthiest language that ever I received of any man to my knowledge."

The tutors were changed, and "Mr. Brown now being Tutor carried so respectfully to us that he had our very hearts, and we scarce did anything without his advice. So long as I remained in College, the Lord gave me the affections of all both in College and in the Town whose love was worth having. Some who spoke me fair, but grudged me my charitable and well grounded esteem of good will being an object of their envy, when on this account I proposed to lay down my place at Commencement, the President by his incessant request and desires prevailed upon me to tarry in it as yet." . . .

"November 17th, 1671. Being quarter day a messenger sent from Westfield to the Bay for to get a minister for that people, being by eight or nine elders met at the

lecture at Boston the day before directed
to myself came to me with a letter from
Mr. Increase Mather, Pastor of the Second
Church at Boston, whom for an answer I
referred to the Rev. President and Fellows,
reserving liberty to advise with friends and
finding Mr. Danforth for it, Mr. Oakes in-
different rather advising to it, the President altogether against it at this time and
the Fellows advising rather to it than anything else giving as a reason why their
advice was not positive because they *were
to respect the College good*, hereupon I was
both encouraged and discouraged, but Mr.
Danforth the Magistrate driving on hard
advised to take other advice, wherefore de-
laying to give an answer to the 21st day,
I did on the 18th advise with Mr. Increase
Mather and Mr. Thacher whose advice was
positive for it."

He accepted the call, and they started on
the 27th November, " not without much

apprehension of a tedious and hazardous journey, the snow being about mid-leg deep, the way unbeaten or the track filled up again over rocks and mountains, the journey being about 100 miles, and Mr. Cooke of Cambridge told us it was the desperatest journey that ever Connecticut men undertook."

" On the night before I went to take my leave of our honored President whose mind was changed, and his love was so much expressed that I could scarce leave him, and he told me in plain words that he knew not how to part with me, but as my proceedings were by prayer and Counsel, so my journey was carried on by mercy and good success.

"The first night we lodged at Malbury, from thence we went out the day following about half an hour before sunrising for Quabaug [Brookfield], but about eleven o'clock we lost our way in the snow and woods, which hindered us some three or four miles, but finding it again by marked trees, on we went but our talk was of lying in the woods all night, for we were then about thirty miles off from our lodging, having neither house nor wigwam on the way, but about eight o'clock at night we came in through mercy in health to our lodgings from which the next day we set out for Springfield, which we arrived at also in health, and on the next day we ventured to lead our horses in great danger over Connecticut river, though altogether against my will, upon the ice which was about two days in freezing, but mercy along with us though the ice cracked every step, yet we came over safely and well to the wonder of all who knew it.

" This being the 1st December we came to Westfield the place of our desire in health where we first called at Capt. Cook's who entertained us with great joy and gladness, giving us many thanks for coming and at such a season. . . ." "The men of the Town came to welcome me," etc. "On Lord's day after I preached to them my first sermon from Matthew 3d Ch. 2d v. being Dec. 3, 1671."

Lockwood says that "Mr. Taylor did not determine for some time to stay, but there being a prospect of organizing a Church, he began to incline to settle." The population was small and the inducements for an educated man to make the place his home for life were few; but "he soon became connected with an event where the interests of this section of the Colony became involved which required his energy, his talent, and his foresight, to conduct to a successful issue." He went to Westfield four years before the breaking out of King Philip's war, during which the inhabitants were kept in a state of excitement and fear. Through the day they labored within reach of their loaded guns or of sentries to give an alarm, and in the night were regularly gathered into the fort, while guards mounted the turrets of the watch-house, etc. The buildings of four families were burned, and several persons were killed or carried away.

No aid was to be expected from the Government. which advised the inhabitants to quit their homes and unite with other towns for more efficient protection. Mr. Taylor and others in behalf of the inhabitants wrote to the State authorities for aid, but were refused with the consoling remark, "Its good doing what we can and leave the rest to God." "To Mr. Taylor's presence and influence it was very much owing that the settlement did not break up."

Preparations for the organization of a church were not made until the spring of 1679. Five churches were invited to convene for the purpose on the 27th August. Four of the five churches were represented, and the then ministers were Peletiah Glover of Springfield, John Russell of Hadley, and Solomon Stoddard of Northampton.

The war was ended, and a minister was settled. New colonists increased the population, etc. The church accommodations became too contracted for the worshipers. It was voted to build a gallery on one side of the meeting house, "to make it comely and comfortable as speedily as may be." Two hundred acres of land were sold to purchase a bell, that the people might no longer be summoned to meeting by beat of drum.

Mr. Taylor discharged the duties of a physician, ministering alike to the bodily and spiritual wants of the population scattered over an extensive territory.

I will here insert his love-letter written "to Miss Elizabeth Fitch," at her father's house in Norwich, dated "8th of 7th month, 1674." The letter was in two parts. The body of the first part was a square inclosing a triangle, and in the center of all a heart. A ring was also drawn upon the paper with the words, "Love's ring I send which has no end."

Rising from the center of the square at the top was a dove of exquisite workmanship holding an olive-branch in its mouth. and these lines were written upon the body of the dove so small as to be scarcely legible.

> This Dove and Olive branch to you
> Is both a Post and emblem too.

There was much more written that was illegible.

WESTFIELD, 8th of 7th month, 1674.
MY DOVE:

I send you not my heart, for that, I hope, is sent to heaven long since, and unless it hath awfully deceived me, it hath not taken up its lodgings in any one's bosom on this side of the royal city of the great King, but yet the most of it that is allowed to be bestowed upon creature, doth solely and singly fall to your share. So much my post pigeon presents you with here in these lines. Look not, I beseech you, upon it as one of love's hyperboles, if I borrow the beams of some sparkling metaphor to illustrate my respect unto thyself by, for you having made my breast the cabinet of your affections as I your's mine, I know not how to offer a fitter comparison to set out my love by, than to compare it to a golden ball of fire, rolling up and down my breast, from which there flies now and then a spark like a glorious beam from the body of the flaming sun, but I, alas, striving to catch these sparks into a love-letter unto thyself, and to guide it as with a sunbeam, find that by what time they have fallen through my pen upon my paper, they have lost their shine and look only like a little smoke thereon instead of gilding it, wherefore finding myself so much discouraged, I am ready to begrudge my instrument for, though my love within my breast is so large that my heart is not sufficient to contain it, yet I can make it no more room to ride in than to squeeze it up betwixt my black ink and white paper, but know that it 's the coarsest part that 's conversant there, for the purest part 's too fine to clothe in any Lingua housewifery to be expressed by words, and this letter bears the coarsest part to you, yet 'he purest is improved

2          17

for you. But now my dear love, lest my letter should be judged the lavish language of a lover's pen, I shall endeavor to show that conjugal love ought to exceed all other love :

1st. It appears from that which it represents, viz : the respect which is between Christ and his Church (Ephesians v. 25) although it differs from that in kind (for that is spiritual and this human), and in a degree that is boundless and transcendent.

2nd. Because conjugal love is the ground of conjugal union.

3rd. From the Christian duties which are incumbent on persons of this state, as not only a serving God together, a praying together, a joining together in the ruling and instructing of their families (which cannot be carried on as it should be without a great degree of true love), a mutual giving each other to each other, and a mutual encouraging each other in all states and grievances. And how can this be when there is not love surmounting all other love ? It 's with them therefore for the most part, as with the strings of an instrument not tuned together, which when struck upon make but a harsh, jarring sound ; but when the golden wires of an instrument, equally drawn up and rightly struck upon, tuned together, make sweet music whose harmony doth enravish the ear, so when the golden strings of true affection are strained up into a right conjugal love, thus doth this state harmonise to the comfort of each other and the glory of God when sanctified. But though conjugal love must exceed all other love, it must be kept within bounds too, for it must be subordinate to God's glory, the which that mine may be so, *it having got you in my heart, doth offer my heart with you in it,* as a more rich sacrifice unto God through Christ, and so it subscribeth me,

Your true love till death,

EDWARD TAYLOR.

It is sometimes said that the old New England Puritans had no poetry in them, but I think that this letter, with its drawings of a heart, ring, and dove, rather tends to disprove such an assertion.

Rev. Edward Taylor and Elizabeth Fitch were married the same year, 1674. She died in 1689, leaving eight children.

Mr. Taylor married, in 1692, Ruth Wyllys of Hartford, Connecticut. She was the daughter of Samuel Wyllys, who was born in 1632, a State Senator for over thirty years, and she was granddaughter of John Haynes, Governor of Massachusetts in 1635, who removed to Hartford, Connecticut, in 1637, was elected first Governor of Connecticut in 1639, and was elected Governor every alternate year until about 1654.

Governor Haynes married, in 1636, Mabel Harlakenden, who it is said came from England for that purpose, both having been born in or near Fenny Compton, England. Of her we read that " she was descended through many lines of Kings and noblemen from William the Conqueror, the first three Henrys, the first three Edwards, John of Gaunt," etc.

Governor Wyllys owned the property in Hartford upon which stood the Charter Oak, and I remember that fifty years ago it still was called " the Wyllys place."

Ruth Wyllys had one son and five daughters.

Hon. Eldad Taylor was the fourteenth and youngest child of Edward Taylor and sixth of Ruth Wyllys. He died in Boston in 1777, while a member of the Provincial Congress and of the Governor's Council, in the sixty-ninth year of his age. The five daughters above mentioned all married clergymen, as follows: Rev. Benjamin Colton of West Hartford; Rev. Ebenezer Devotion of Suffield; Rev. Benjamin Lord of Norwich; Rev. William Gager of Lebanon; Rev. Isaac Stiles of North Haven, father of President Stiles of Yale College.

Rev. John Taylor was the fourteenth child of Hon. Eldad Taylor and Thankful Day of West Springfield. He was settled at Deerfield for about nineteen years as pastor, and dropped suddenly while preaching in his pulpit. He recovered, but lost his voice for many years, finally regaining it sufficiently to preach occasionally, but never again as pastor. It is recorded of him that he was a man of great ability as a preacher of the Gospel, and I have many of his manuscript sermons which tend to prove this. I heard him preach one sermon in Hartford about 1828, from the text, "Unto you that fear my name shall the Sun of righteousness arise with healing in his wings"; and although then but a child, I have never forgotten it. He was married at Enfield. Connecticut, to Elizabeth Terry.

The reader of this will have observed that Rev. John Taylor was grandson of Rev. Edward Taylor and sixth in direct descent from Governor John Haynes and Mabel Harlakenden. His wife, Elizabeth Terry, was also sixth in direct descent from Governor William Bradford of the Mayflower, as follows, viz. :

Her father was Colonel Nathaniel Terry of Enfield and Abiah Dwight. He was the son of Major Ephraim Terry and Ann Collins. She was daughter of Rev. Nathaniel

THE children of Rev. John Taylor and Elizabeth Terry, whose marriage is mentioned on page 23, were as follows, viz.: Elizabeth, born 1789; married the Rev. James Taylor, of Sunderland, Mass. Jabez Terry, born 1790; married Esther Allen, of Enfield, Conn. John, born 1792, of Bruce, Mich.; married Phebe Leach. Harriet, born 1794; married Roderick Terry, of Hartford, Conn. Henry Wyllys, born 1796, of Canandaigua, N. Y.; married Martha C. Masters. Mary, born 1798; married Josiah Wright, of Syracuse, N. Y. Nathaniel Terry, born 1800; married Laura Winchell. And four children who died in early infancy.

In the last clause upon page 22 it is printed, "Her father was Colonel Nathaniel Terry and Abiah Dwight." It should read, "She was the daughter of Colonel Nathaniel Terry and Abiah Dwight."

Collins (pastor at Enfield) and Alice Adams.
Alice Adams was daughter of Rev. W.
Adams and Alice Bradford. Alice B. was
daughter of Hon. William Bradford and
Alice Richard, and William B. was son of
Governor William Bradford of the May-
flower. So that in the marriage of Rev.
John Taylor and Elizabeth Terry we have the
Pilgrim and the Puritan descendants allied.

The news of the battle of Lexington
reached Enfield, Connecticut, on Sunday, and
on Monday following the Nathaniel Terry
named above left Enfield for Boston as captain in command of fifty-nine men. He
continued engaged during the War of the
Revolution as captain, major, quartermas-
ter, and colonel. He was a man of wealth,
and sacrificed almost all his property in the
patriot cause.

The descendants of the Rev. John Taylor are related by blood to the following

presidents of Yale College : President Stiles, President Day, and President Woolsey. The wife of President Clapp was also a granddaughter of Rev. Edward Taylor. Elizabeth Terry, his wife, was also distantly related to both the Presidents Dwight. I may also state that Samuel Terry, one of her ancestors, was patentee of the town of Enfield.

To return to the Rev. Edward Taylor, a communication from Westfield in the "Boston News-Letter" says he died 14th June, 1729, in the eighty-seventh year of his age, "and what a rich blessing God sent us in him, almost 58 years experience has taught us. . . . He was eminently holy in his life and very painful [?] and laborious in his work, till the infirmities of great old age disabled him. He continued to have the sole oversight of his flock till Oct. 26th, 1726, when the Rev. Mr. Bull was ordained among us, in which solemn action he bore his part."

Judge Sewall writes, 18th April, 1728 : " The Rev. Mr. Taylor of Westfield sits in his great chair, and cannot walk to his bed without support. He is longing and waiting for his dismission."

A tombstone still stands in the old burying-ground at Westfield with this inscription : "Here rests the body of ye Rev. Mr. Edward Taylor ye aged, venerable, learned and pious pastor of ye Church of Christ in this town, who after he had served God and his generation faithfully for many years fell asleep June 24th 1729 in ye 87th year of his age."

His grandson, President Stiles of Yale College, says that " Mr. Taylor was very curious in Botany, and different branches of Natural History, an incessant student, but used no spectacle glasses to his death. He was a vigorous advocate for Oliver Cromwell, civil and religious liberty. A Congregationalist in opposition to Presbyterian

Church discipline. He was a physician for the town all his life. He concerned himself little about domestic and secular affairs. He greatly detested King James, Sir Edmond Andross and Randolph, and gloried in King William and the Revolution of 1688. He was exemplary in piety and for a very sacred observance of the Lord's Day."

Nearly all his professional books, which he had transcribed as he had opportunity, were in manuscript. His manuscripts were all handsomely bound by himself in parchment, of which tradition says he left at his death more than a hundred volumes in prose and poetry. Fourteen of these were in quarto. Before his death he prohibited their publication.

His library descended to his grandson, President Stiles, and many of the manuscripts were given by President Stiles and his father, Rev. Isaac Stiles, to the library of Yale College.

# RUTH TAYLOR AND HER FIVE DAUGHTERS.

BY EMMA C. NASON.

IT was long, long ago, in the rustic old days
When the spinning-wheel's hum was the music of
   home,
Accompanied maybe by caroling lays,
But oftener still by the clattering loom.

THERE were fourteen children in all in the family, and thirteen of them were girls. We have not the names nor the history of all this constellation of sisters, but, judging from what we know, we expect, when all the beautiful daughters of Zion are gathered, that there will be found those faithful sisters who in obscure places have contributed to the light of the perfect day.

The children of the Taylor family were all cradled in the arms of faith, and all knelt by the side of a Christian mother. The father was Rev. Edward Taylor, a New England minister, living in Westfield. Mass. But the girls did not all belong to the same mother.

Ruth Taylor was a stepmother. Eight of the little ones were not her own, although her tender faithfulness was added to the precious legacy of love that the departed mother had left them. Elizabeth, the first wife, was the daughter of Rev. James Fitch, of Norwich, Conn., and the granddaughter of Rev. Henry Whitfield, of Guilford. The first chapter of the family history is briefly told.

Edward Taylor, a Harvard graduate of 1671, just as he had received college honors, was called by an urgent message to a new settlement on the extreme outpost of civilization. He unhesitatingly accepted the call, and in the early winter crossed the Massachusetts forest, guided "a great part of the way by marked trees." The settlement was exposed to great danger. Every night the few inhabitants were gathered into the fort for safety, and through the day they labored constantly within reach of their firearms. After three years the young minister won a brave-hearted bride, to share the dangers and the poverty of his frontier cabin life.

A heroic heart, a wealth of love and faith, both human and divine, had Elizabeth. Fifteen years she stood by his side, braving the dangers and enduring hardships. The perils which hung over them were at times truly appalling. "The hardships were equalled only by the heroism they inspired." Amid the terrors of King Philip's war their

first babes were cradled.  But the protect-
ing wings of Providence shielded their
home.  The fifteen years passed.  Eight
young souls had awakened in the cabin
parsonage.  The dangers of the first Indian
war had passed, but while the settlers hoped
for long years of peace, again was heard
the war-whoop of the savage.  But in this
home death, by unseen hand of disease,
preceded the more dreaded foe.  The mother was taken.  Imagination must picture the desolation of that hearthstone.
Added to its poverty, added to all its ex-
posures, was now the cry of bleeding hearts
for the mother and the companion gone
forever.

It became the mission of Ruth Wyllys, of
Hartford, to fill the vacant place.  It was a
great responsibility—a far greater one than
Elizabeth Fitch had taken.  The dangers
were hardly less, grim want had kept step
with the increase of the family, while the

household cares were multiplied. The minister had already reached middle life, and as his own burdens were heavy, very much must fall upon his young companion. To his work as pastor had been added the duties of a physician, and in his double vocation he was the servant of a population extended over a large territory. Thus it will be readily seen that no easy life allured the young bride on her slow wedding tour up the Connecticut. How different from the modern wedding tour was that, and at the end of the journey a cabin full of little girls, and the daily problem to be solved. "What shall we eat and drink, and wherewithal shall we be clothed?"

Ruth Taylor entered upon her work in 1692, the year made memorable by the outbreak of the witchcraft excitement. But the weird rumors of the Salem witchcraft, with its lamentable results, were to these frontier people of less significance than the startling stories that reached them ever and anon that the cruel savages were on the war-path. The most vivid imagination can hardly picture those times. Truth is stranger than fiction. Ruth Taylor needed not to read the latter, her own life was story enough. To the household of daughters there were added one by one her own five girls.

First came baby Ruth, the mother's precious namesake, the child who walked in the mother's footsteps, the daughter who on her bridal journey retraced her mother's own path down the Connecticut, and at West Hartford spent the wealth of her beautiful years, leaving in the parish of her husband her great influence; extending it into Massachusetts again in the life of her son, and reaching it on and on in pious posterity down to our own time.

The next born was little Naomi. Was it for Ruth's mother that she was named?

this dear daughter whose works in womanhood were to praise her in the gates of
Suffield; whose influence in another generation was, through her son, to extend
over the walls of Windham; broaden still
wider, a generation later, from the Saybrook platform, and, running on through
another channel, reach Coventry; and
again, westward bound, be recognized in
Ohio in the halls of justice, and later still
in the office of chief magistrate of the State.

Who can set the bounds of influence?
Who can measure the length and breadth
and height thereof? Ruth Taylor could
not know the future of her girls. The
best she could do was to nurture them
for the Lord and trust him.

Anne, her third daughter, and eleventh
of the family, was born in the year 1697.
Could another girl be welcome when the
narrow cabin was already full and running
over? Every babe brought so much added

care that doubtless the poor, toil-worn mother at times almost fainted.

Had the precious infant, Anne Taylor, been sacrificed to domestic convenience, fifty-two years of a useful life had not been. We shall yet see how that half-century was wrought in golden woof in God's glorious plan, while the web of life went on in her five children, and on still, in children's children, to present generations.

Next to Anne came Mehitable, or Hetta, who was to be another luminary in the constellation of sisters.

The last, and the thirteenth, baby girl of the Taylor family was Keziah. The mission of the bright Kezzy was soon finished, yet she lived long enough to become the center of a new home and to receive the crown of motherhood, leaving in her nursery a jewel for the Master that would one day be acknowledged a light of the first magnitude.

After the troop of girls there came one baby boy to occupy the cabin cradle — one son among thirteen daughters! What a large amount of petting must have been bestowed on the little fellow, the pride of his gray-haired father, the delight of his loving mother, the pet of a whole houseful of sisters, and the infant hero of the parish! The wonder is that the boy Eldad was not spoiled, and the fact that he was not of itself speaks well for the thorough discipline of the Taylor household. This son alone, of all his father's family, could transmit the family name to after generations; and Eldad Taylor was not recreant to that good name, but grew up among his dozen sisters, sharing lavishly their affection, and filled with the noble spirit of those pure hearts, ready at last to go forth and spread the influence of the family with the name he bore.

We regret that we cannot trace the influence of Ruth Taylor in the lives of the large group of stepdaughters that she helped to fit for their work; but, looking at the family picture in the far distance, we can see only those that history has placed in the foreground, and must content ourselves with the thought that when the light of the perfect day shall fall upon the whole canvas these workers will appear in distinct view. But history gives us just a glimpse of the addition of one of the interesting group surrounding Ruth Taylor. The eldest stepdaughter married early, and died leaving an infant daughter. This motherless little one was immediately received into the Westfield home and adopted as their very own. Think of it! ye mothers at ease, who shun the responsibility of your own family; think of Ruth with all her baby girls, who crowded so fast into the narrow parsonage, yet giving room, freely, to the child of her stepdaughter, and giving to it the love it craved in her motherly heart. In that hour a fresh benediction rested upon her home. This new immortal would complete the mother's final crown of rejoicing. The child grew up with the five little aunties, sharing every way with them while there awaited her a sphere of future usefulness every way similar to their own.

Thus Ruth Taylor's daughters were counted at last six instead of five. And when they had grown to beautiful womanhood, through a remarkable providence, six young ministers, all from Connecticut, were attracted, one by one, to the Westfield parsonage, and from that loving circle each young servant of the Master won for himself a companion.

Ruth, the eldest, married Rev. Benjamin Colton, of West Hartford.

Naomi followed as the bride of Rev. Ebenezer Devotion, of Suffield.

Anne went forth to a happy home with Rev. Benjamin Lord, D. D., of Norwich.

Hetta became the loving helpmeet of Rev. William Gager, of Lebanon.

Kezzy, in her short mission of love, blessed the home of Rev. Isaac Stiles, of North Haven.

Last, the adopted daughter went forth to the work of the Master with Rev. Peter Reynolds, the young minister of Enfield.

In the six different parishes they labored simultaneously, and the work of Ruth Taylor's daughters became known in the gates, from the center field to the borders of old Connecticut. Would we number the sheaves of the faithful mother Ruth? We must first learn the history of West Hartford, and know how much Ruth Colton contributed to the plentiful harvest there; we must follow the results, also, in the field of their son, Rev. George Colton, of Bolton, Mass., whose devout life reached down to 1812;

and then we must pursue our investigation on through all the branches of Ruth Colton's family.

Next we must turn to the sister Naomi, and in her husband's vineyard at Suffield read the story of their united toil, finding the continuation of that story in the faithfulness of their son, Rev. Ebenezer Devotion, Jr., of Windham, Conn., and again continued in his son, Rev. John Devotion, of Saybrook, and on down through his family. Then the work takes us to Coventry, Conn., where we find John Devotion's sister united in labor with Rev. Joseph Huntington; and another sequel is found in their ten children, one of whom, Hon. Samuel Huntington, removes to Ohio and becomes Chief Justice of the State, and afterward its Governor. His family would take us still onward; but we return to his sister, Frances Huntington, who married Rev. Edward D. Griffin, D. D., so emi-

nently known in his pastoral labors in
Newark, N. J., and Park Street, Boston, and
who was fifteen years President of Williams
College, also one of the founders of the
American Bible Society, and connected
with almost every benevolent enterprise of
his day ; in all of which relations his devoted
and accomplished wife was found closely
associated with him, their daughters also
occupying stations of usefulness. One of
these, well known as the wife of Dr. L. N.
Smith, of Newark, fell a martyr to her own
work of love, "a lady of the finest intellec-
tual and moral qualities, distinguished alike
in authorship and philanthropy." And
through all these channels and many more
may be traced indirectly the influence of
Naomi Devotion.

Next we turn to Anne Lord, of Norwich.
But what amount of study will ever be able
to compute the outgrowth of the work of
Rev. Dr. Lord and his devout companion,

during those revival years of the eighteenth century when the Norwich church, that could hardly be reckoned by the score, became multiplied to hundreds? A mountain in the history of Norwich stands the work of Dr. Benjamin Lord, and from the base to the summit of that mountain may be traced the footprints of his wife, Anne. And when she had finished her half-century course, and received her reward, there are still to be numbered the sheaves of her five children in the field, and of their descendants.

Then we must hasten over to Lebanon to acquaint ourselves with the work of Mehitable, that "gift of the Lord" to Rev. Wm. Gager. But we here become lost in our hasty reckoning. As well might we try to number the deep, wide-spread roots of the tall cedars of ancient Lebanon, as to reckon the influences of their Christian home in Central Connecticut. Verily the old prophecy hastens to fulfilment, "An handful of corn in the earth, upon the top of the mountains, and the fruit thereof shall shake like Lebanon." We find the fruit of the Taylor family already amounting to a sum that can only be reckoned by the mathematics of heaven, and yet we cannot pause in our outlook on the harvests.

Kezzy Stiles presents her quickly gathered sheaves. A happy bride in the beautiful June of 1725, and only a year and a half later, in bleak December, a dying young mother, who in the parsonage at North Haven gives her life for the frailest of infant sons. That babe, whose slender existence hardly whispered the faintest breath of hope to bleeding hearts, was all that remained of the beautiful Kezzy's life that had promised so much. All! But God sees all, not as mortals see it. Just fifty years passed, and the only child of that mother was known as Rev. Ezra Stiles, D. D.,

President of Yale College. Of him, Chancellor Kent has said, " Take him all in all, this extraordinary man was undoubtedly one of the purest and best-gifted men of his age."

President Stiles was the father of eight children, but we cannot follow these descendants. Neither have we space to note the greatness of the work at Enfield, where during forty-four years Rev. Peter Reynolds and his beloved companion won jewels for the kingdom. The final day shall declare it, how this last daughter of the Taylors, the child of the first, was the finishing glory of the brilliant crown of Ruth Taylor. But her daughters were not her only jewels. Her one son grew up to honor her, and while his sisters served the church, he served as faithfully the state. He fell at his post, an honored Senator of Massachusetts, during the War of Independence. And in places of trust in our nation are still to

be found the descendants of Hon. Eldad
Taylor.  In the fields of church and state
who shall reckon the sheaves of Ruth?

# MORE ABOUT RUTH TAYLOR, HER ANCESTORS AND DESCENDANTS.

NOTE.— In our late sketch of this mother, we made some misstatements, to which we had been led by errors that had slipped into history. Through the kindness of Hon. Henry W. Taylor, of Canandaigua, New-York, we are able to make these corrections. Ruth's maiden name, instead of being spelled Wyll*i*s (as it is given in Sprague's "Annals"), is Wyll*y*s, the spelling having been changed after the family came to America. This correction might be of little account, were it not for the important aid it gives in tracing a family whose sons have been distinguished, and whose daughters have been "corner-stones." The other mistake is more significant in its relation to fact. Rev. Edward Taylor, instead of having *eight* daughters in his first marriage, had three sons and only five daughters. His two eldest children were Samuel and James, who lived to manhood; the youngest was Hezekiah, who died young. The granddaughter, who was adopted by Ruth, instead of being the child of his eldest daughter, as is stated in the "Annals," was the only child of the eldest son, Samuel. We regret that it has been necessary to make these corrections, yet we are glad, in the interest of history, to be able to do so. In these sketches we try to have all our statements based upon the best authority, but the threads of family history are sometimes to be traced only by the most careful research. Little, comparatively, has been written about the Wyllys and Taylor families; families which through all their branches have had a remarkable number of eminent descendants. Like mountain-peaks, these individual lives have stood in history, but they have not been connected into a mountain-chain. The neglect is to be regretted; and if our humble sketch of this mother Ruth shall, even with its mistakes, call forth facts, in the possession of living descendants, which have never before been given to the public, and thereby furnish important connections in the historic chain, our first expectations will be more than realized. Any such information will be gratefully received, either by the writer or by Judge Taylor, who is the nearest living descendant of Rev. Edward and Ruth Taylor. Besides the corrections mentioned he has furnished us with many additional facts of interest, part of which we will give our readers in the sketches to follow.

THE story of Ruth's ancestors is not less interesting than is the history of her descendants.

She was the granddaughter of two Connecticut governors. Her maternal grandfather was John Haynes, Governor of Massachusetts in 1635, and who joined the emigrant party of Rev. Thomas Hooker in 1636, Governor Haynes being, according to Bancroft, the leader of Hooker's party through the forest wilderness of Massachusetts. He was made the first governor of Connecticut, and was reëlected every alternate year until his death, in 1654.

When he came to America, in 1633, he was a widower, but not far from the time of his journey to Connecticut, he married Mabel Harlakenden, who came from England in 1635. We are not informed whether Mabel was one of Hooker's famous company, but it is not unlikely that in this party she went on her bridal tour to her future home. There is no doubt but if the story of Mabel Haynes could be fully told, it would in thrilling truth surpass any modern novel. She was the descendant of kings and of the daughters of English nobility. We are told that her ancestry has been traced back through thirteen different lines to William the Conqueror. It is probable that no other maiden ever came over with the Puritans, whose ancestry could be traced so far, and through so many royal names. Reared in luxury, Mabel and her brother Roger left their sumptuous English home,—Roger being the proprietor of a grand park of 1800 acres in England,— left all this beautiful estate to face the untried hardships of the American wilderness. Roger soon died, and Mabel, "the daughter of nobility," gave the wealth of her life to Connecticut. The new colony needed just such female heroism as was displayed by the Governor's young wife.

The name of John Haynes is venerated in history, and the name of the ardent, loving Mabel should be given its own place beside it ; and glad are we to introduce her to our readers as the beloved grandmother of Ruth Wyllys Taylor. We cannot fail to observe the family likeness between them, and we almost involuntarily repeat the proverb, "As is the mother, so is her daughter."

Ruth Haynes, the daughter of Mabel, married the son of Governor George Wyllys. The home of the Governor, one of the finest situations in Hartford, known as the " Wyllys Place," came into the possession of the son, Hon. Samuel Wyllys, and here, in this picturesque spot, were born Ruth

Taylor, her two sisters and brother Hezekiah. Her father, when only twenty-two years old, was elected to the upper house of the Connecticut Legislature, to which honorable position he was returned by annual elections, without intermission, for thirty years, until the time when Sir Edmund Andros usurped the reins of government. Thus the son of Governor Wyllys was constantly busy in the legislative halls; but meanwhile the daughter of Governor Haynes was the faithful "keeper at home," and the beautiful "Wyllys Place" was a nursery for church and state. Around this early home of Ruth Taylor are grouped many of the most thrilling scenes in the history of Hartford. "The old oak" in front of the house, under whose branches Ruth and the other children played, was afterward to become the most famous tree in America, so famous as to be made a universal medium for advertising an "insurance," "giving a name to everything, from a great banking-house down to a box of blacking." Irresistibly are we carried back to those days when the English usurper demanded the beloved Charter of Connecticut. In imagination we stand in Hartford on that memorable day in the autumn of 1687, when the din of arms proclaims that the time of final decision has come. Andros, with sixty soldiers, marches into town and demands the charter. Will the heroes of Hartford yield? They meet in general council to consider. The Assembly is held in the Old Church. Of course, Ruth's father is there, but at home the mother with the children, Hezekiah, a boy of fifteen, the thoughtful Ruth, and her sisters, all are intensely interested. We take our place with them —the house is close by the Assembly— and we watch the building surrounded by soldiers. But hour after hour the debate continues. The sun sets. The dark curtain of night falls, while every heart is still in suspense. The candle-lights flicker from the old church, and the thick darkness without increases—when, suddenly, the church is as dark as the night without. Confusion follows, and soon the story spreads on wings over Hartford, "The charter is gone." Just as the tyrant hand was stretched out to grasp it, the light of every candle in a twinkling went out, and in the sudden darkness, noise, and confusion the precious charter disappeared. Where was it? That was a Hartford secret. It was guarded well. The friendly old oak opposite Ruth's home never whispered it, but for twenty long months it kept the valuable treasure concealed in its bosom. That memorable night was five years before Ruth's marriage, and Ruth, when the dangers were passed, celebrated with the rest of the family the happy May-day in 1689, when the charter was taken from the trunk of the old oak, when the government was restored, and Ruth's father was again given his place in the Legislature. Hon. Samuel Wyllys served six years more, making a total of thirty-six years in this office. But the sequel of this family's official history is still more remarkable. Hezekiah, the only brother of Ruth, was elected in 1711 Secretary of State, and by annual elections was continued in this office for twenty-three years, until his death. His immediate successor as Secretary was his own son George Wyllys, who was elected annually to the office for sixty-one years, until his death, in 1795, when he was succeeded by his son, General Samuel Wyllys, who was elected every year, for fifteen years, until 1809, the office of Secretary of State having thus been during ninety-nine consecutive years by annual elections given to Ruth's brother, his son, and grandson. Adding to this the thirty-six years that Ruth's father served in the Legislature, and the time that her grandfather, Governor Wyllys, held the office, either of chief magistrate or as assistant in Connecticut, and we have a record of one hundred and forty-one years, where high places of trust were annually given by the people to the Wyllys family. Is there to be found anywhere an official history similar to this?

Our readers have now become somewhat acquainted with Ruth's ancestors, have lingered near her childhood home, have recognized the old charter-oak as it stood a sentinel, as it were, over "the Wyllys place," and guarded in its secret treasury the most liberal grant that had ever issued from the royal hand; bounding the Connecticut colony on the west by the Pacific Ocean, and thus preparing the

54

way of the American nation for its wide claim to the great Western States of our Union. Well might the Wyllys family cherish and our whole people venerate that grand old oak! We have followed also the boy Hezekiah, who whistled beneath its shade and climbed to its topmost branches. Taking a look into the distance, we have seen Connecticut intrusting for a century its important records to the faithful Hezekiah and his family.

Now we go back and follow again the maiden Ruth. We are better prepared than we were at first to follow this descendant of kings, this granddaughter of two governors, who, like the brave-hearted Mabel, counted not the hardships before her. We realize more than at first how great the change from the Wyllys place in Hartford to the cabin parsonage of Westfield. But the minister's motherless children were waiting for the blessing

55

of her life. The two boys, Samuel and James, were just at the age when boys need, perhaps, more than at any other time, the gentle influence of a judicious mother; and the influence that was so blessed in the training of their younger sisters must have fallen with a precious benediction upon the minister's boys. Their sister, Bathsheba, was nine years old when the stepmother came, and Elizabeth was between seven and eight. Mary, Abigail, and the other sister died young, and Hezekiah, their little brother, was also numbered with the early dead.

Samuel and James grew up to manhood, and the two brothers went into the mercantile business together; but Samuel, while absent in the West Indies, died suddenly, and, not far from the same time, James died at home. Thus, almost at one stroke, the minister's family was bereft of its sons. The only one finally to perpetuate the family name was the boy Eldad, who followed in the wake of his ten sisters. Samuel had married, but his young wife died before he did, leaving only an infant daughter, Elizabeth, the adopted one of the Taylor household, who grew up with Ruth's little ones. But before we follow the history of this child and Ruth's daughters further, let us turn to the half-sisters, Bathsheba and Elizabeth. They were educated almost entirely under the loving watch-care of their stepmother; and while assisting her in the household duties, and rocking the cradle of the little ones, they grew in all the domestic graces, and beneath the culture of the wise young mother developed into lovely womanhood. But death claimed the beautiful Elizabeth for his bride, before any happy suitor had won her from the parsonage. Judge Taylor says, in reference to her: "In my early youth the traditions of Elizabeth were clear

and bright.   She died, I believe, at the age
of eighteen or twenty.   According to tradition, she was ·an extraordinarily gifted
and lovely girl.   It is said that no person
had ever died in Westfield whose death had
caused such universal and profound grief.''
Who shall tell what an influence for good
may have followed this lovely life?

The fair Bathsheba now alone was left
of all the first mother's daughters to carry
the influence of the Taylor household into
a home of her own.   Hon. John Pynchon,
a young man of worth, received this first
bride of the parsonage.   He was a descendant also of Governor Wyllys, his grandfather, Colonel John Pynchon, having married the Governor's daughter, Amy Wyllys,
the aunt of Ruth Taylor.   Thus the descendants of the stepdaughter came in Ruth's
own line of descent.   The Pynchon family
had received well-merited honor for their
public spirit, skill, and faithfulness in every

position they filled.   The son-in-law of the
Westfield minister was prepared by his up-
right predecessors to extend the family influence in his union with Bathsheba.   Her
life was not long, yet was lengthened until
she had nursed a flock of precious little
ones for the Master, and then some one
else was raised up to carry on her work.
We must pass over those years, when, in
the household of Bathsheba, the life of the
Taylor nursery was repeated, and content
ourselves by pointing our readers to a few
of the results.

We cannot attempt more than an imperfect glance.   The family circle has become
far extended.   It would take many volumes
to tell all the story of Bathsheba Pynchon,
her seven or eight children, and their descendants.   We would need to learn the
record of her son, Joseph Pynchon, the Harvard graduate of 1726, and know all the
great family history of her daughter, Eliza-

beth Pynchon, who married a Mr. Colton, and had fifteen children, nine sons and six daughters ; and still another volume would be needed to trace the sister, Bathsheba, who married Robert Harris, and from whom, according to Dr. Sprague, descended President Harris, of Columbia College. But the mother Bathsheba's multiplied life would not be half portrayed, even then. You must learn by the most thorough acquaintance the remarkable family history of her daughte., Mary Pynchon, who married General Joseph Dwight, and had nine children. Study then the saintly life of their daughter, Lydia Dwight. who married Rev. John Willard. from whom have descended many eminent clergymen, and such men in official life as Hon. John Dwight Willard.

Another volume of the life of Mary Pynchon Dwight is that of her daughter, Dorothy, who married Hon. Jedediah Foster, a Judge of the Supreme Court of Massachusetts, and a member of the convention which framed the constitution of that State. The history is still continued in the life of their son, Judge Dwight Foster, a United States Senator from Massachusetts. Add to this the life of Hon. Theodore Foster, another Senator, for thirteen years, from Rhode Island ; include in the catalogue the life of General Dwight Foster, another Judge of the Supreme Court, and forget not to embrace the noble record of Alfred Dwight Foster, of Worcester, Massachusetts. What a library it would take to tell all the story of the Pynchons, the Coltons, the Harrises, the Dwights, the Willards, and the Fosters, descendants of Bathsheba ! We have named only a few of the many who are included in this family. Besides all its renowned senators and judges, ministers, professors, and college presidents, now placed on high, how many faithful Elizabeths, noble Bathshebas, loving Marys, saintly Dorothys, and beloved Lydias,— a host of true-hearted Christian women,— descendants of Bathsheba Taylor, the step-daughter of Ruth.

We turn again to Ruth's own girls. We have followed her eldest daughter, Ruth, to West Hartford, and have had a faint view of the influence she exerted in her union with Rev. Benjamin Colton and their children. A question has arisen whether Rev. George Colton, of Massachusetts, was their son or not, as some of the family have not his name on their records ; but Judge Taylor is inclined to think this only an omission, and that our statement, taken from history, is correct, as he remembers that his own father often mentioned with his relatives Rev. George Colton, who, on account of his great height, was called the "high priest." We are also informed that Rev.

Ely Colton, of Stratford, Conn., was reckoned among the sons of the West Hartford parsonage, and besides there was a son Benjamin.

Ruth Colton had a daughter, a namesake, who married Timothy Skinner, and Mrs. Ruth Skinner had a Ruth, who became the wife of Rev. Nathaniel Hooker, of West Hartford. We are thus able to trace five generations of Ruths, from the time when Ruth Haynes, the Governor's daughter, let her light shine brightly from the Wyllys home, on the beautiful " hill of Hartford."

Going back to Ruth Colton, we meet another daughter, Thedocia Colton, who joins her life with Rev. Adonijah Bidwell, the first pastor of the church in Tyringham, Mass. We are told that the fair Thedocia was " a poetess," but we believe that her poems were not preserved — women had not yet been given their place among authors.  Traditions of her writings were handed down, but her beautiful life was a brief sonnet, including only seven years of wedded happiness.  To fill her place, Rev. Mr. Bidwell chose her cousin. Jemima Devotion, a daughter of Naomi Taylor.

The history of the Devotion family has called forth close investigation.  It appears that Naomi Taylor was the second wife of Rev. Ebenezer Devotion, of Suffield, and stepmother to the minister's eldest son, who was afterward known as Rev. Ebenezer Devotion, Jr., of Windham, Conn. Although not Naomi's own child, he received from his sixth year the lasting impress of her loving care, growing up under the same influence that was thrown around Rev. John Devotion, of Saybrook, who, we learn, was Naomi's own son, instead of a grandson, as we were at first informed.  Naomi's eldest daughter married Rev. Hezekiah Bissell.  This daughter was the mother of nine children. To her family belonged Colonel Hezekiah Bissell, of East Windsor, whose daughter married Rev. Abel Flint, D. D., of Hartford. Their daughter became the wife of Rev. Herman Norton. Two of Naomi's daughters we are not able to trace, only to learn that one married Jonathan Goodhere, and the other Jonathan Wells. The youngest daughter, Jemima Devotion, who took her cousin Thedocia's place at Tyringham, had four children. Her two sons, Adonijah Bidwell, Jr., and Barnabas, have very many descendants, some of whom have risen to prominent places. One of Jemima's daughters married Eliab Brown. and their son, Rev. Josiah Brown, was for many years missionary in Greece and Asia Minor. The other daughter, Jemima, became the wife of Wm. Partridge, and from the home of Jemima Partridge one of the first missionaries to the Sandwich Islands received his heroic companion. This descendant of Ruth Taylor, Nancy (Partridge) Whitney, was in 1868 still to be found at the Hawaiian Mission, among the remnant of that first brave band who planted the Gospel in the benighted isles of the Pacific. In opposite' directions, the great-grandchildren of Naomi had gone into the mission-field, and in their work they almost met in the circumference of the great vineyard. One of the family wrote years ago : " The children of Jemima Devotion are found in all parts of the world."

We are not able to follow so far the descendants of Anne Taylor, but we doubt not that the work of Rev. Benjamin Lord, D. D., and his devout companion, which stands as a monument in the history of Norwich, Conn., has sent out, in numberless channels, good streams that, flowing on and on, are bearing precious freight to the boundless ocean of eternity. Anne

Lord had four sons, Benjamin, Elihu, Ebenezer, and Joseph. The last two were
twins, and were graduates together at Yale
in 1758.

There are doubtless many descendants
of this Norwich family. One great-grandson of Anne has lately been traced to his
field of labor at Colorado Springs, Col.,
where Rev. Willis Lord is found planting a
new vineyard for the Master.

Hetta Talyor's life cannot be followed
through children's children. The home
of Rev. Wm. Gager, although blessed, was
also afflicted. Their two children were
taken while young to the upper fold.
Mysterious are the ways of Providence.
This mother in Lebanon was written child-
less, and in North Haven her sister Kezzy
left the frailest of infants motherless. But
we have followed the little one until we
have been introduced to the man of great
influence known far and near as President

Stiles, of Yale. The President had two sons
and six daughters. The eldest son, Ezra
Stiles, became a lawyer of North Carolina.
Isaac was at sea at the time of his father's
death, and as he was never afterward heard
from, it was supposed that the ship was
lost in a storm. Elizabeth, the President's
oldest daughter, died about the same time.

Keziah married Hon. Lewis Burr Sturgis,
a member of Congress. Amelia, after her
father's death, had a home for some time
in the family of Rev. John Taylor, the
father of Judge Taylor. She married Hon.
Jonathan Leavitt, of Greenfield, Mass., a
judge of the higher court. She had three
daughters and one son. The latter died
in the midst of his college days. Sarah
Leavitt, the eldest daughter. married a
lawyer ; Mary remained single, and occu-
pied the old home in Greenfield ; Amelia
married a Mr. Jenkins, and their only son
is well known as Rev. Jonathan L. Jenkins,

pastor of the First Church in Pittsfield, Mass.

Ruth Stiles married John M. Gannett, and was the mother of the late Rev. Ezra Stiles Gannett, of Boston. Mary Stiles, the other daughter of the President, was the first wife of Rev. Abiel Holmes, D. D., the father of Oliver Wendell Holmes.

Thus we may trace in high positions, in church and state, the descendants of Keziah Taylor, who lived only long enough to give her child to the world. Elizabeth Taylor, the adopted child of Ruth, has also had numbered among her descendants men high in position. Among these was Hon. James Dixon, late United States Senator from Connecticut, who was a great-grandson of Rev. Peter Reynolds and Elizabeth Taylor.

We have now followed Ruth Taylor's girls from Bathsheba, the stepdaughter, down to the adopted grandchild. We have tried to so trace them, that our readers may follow them still farther, should they know their families. But we must not close our imperfect review without one look at the family of Ruth's only son, Eldad, the youngest of the fourteen children of the Westfield parsonage.

It was the year 1708 when Eldad, the fourteenth child of the parsonage was born, the same year when the little grandchild, Elizabeth, was received into the crowded nursery at Westfield. The death of Samuel's young wife being soon followed by his own death and that of his brother James, the orphaned babe was doubly precious for the sake of the lost; while the blow that suddenly bereft the household of the two grown-up sons led them to fold very closely to their hearts the infant Eldad, the only boy now of the parsonage. But the care to Ruth, at this time, must have been great. When these two children were added to the family, the Westfield pastor was already an old man, his locks well sprinkled with the gray of sixty-six years. Would the Benjamin of his old age prove a staff in his last days? Their hopes were fulfilled. Eldad was their stay. He remained when his five sisters, one by one, went forth to bless the homes of Connecticut ministers; and, when the sixth minister came and took Elizabeth also, the old parsonage had only Eldad left, of all the fifteen children who had gladdened it. Its last blessing was reserved for the noble young son who was its crowning joy. Upon this strong, faithful arm the aged pastor leaned until his feet had touched the last sands on the shore of time. When death divided them the pilgrim had entered his eighty-eighth year, and Eldad had only just reached his majority. Upon the threshold of twenty-one, he received the dying blessing of the patriarch of Westfield. Verily, Eldad Taylor was blessed. How long he was permitted to minister to his beloved mother we know not, but we are sure that by her influence Ruth Taylor remained long as a ministering spirit to her boy. He continued to occupy the old home, where every association was precious. He became a deacon in the church where his father had so long ministered.

We pass over the many years of faithfulness that intervened, and come down to the commencement of the Revolution, when we find in the memorable Senate of Massachusetts Hon. Eldad Taylor. He was selected as one of the Governor's Council. At the close of the legislative session he had a strong desire to return home, but " he was earnestly urged by the Governor to remain and aid him in the threatening emergency." He did so, and fell at his post, as truly a martyr to the cause as the soldiers who gave their lives. Had he returned to Westfield he might have escaped the fatal pestilence, but, obedient to duty, the Massachusetts Senator fell in Boston, by the hand of that dreadful scourge, smallpox, on the 21st of May, 1777. He had been twice married, and left a large family. His first wife, Rhoda Dewey, had five children, but only two survived her. He next married Thankful Day, a relative of President Day, and also of Secretary Thomas, the successor of Secretary Wyllys. Thankful was evidently one of those noble helpers for whom the world outside of her own family has reason to be "thankful." She was the mother of nine children. Thus, it will be noticed, the second Taylor family of the Westfield homestead numbered the same as did the first — fourteen children. At his death,

Hon. Eldad Taylor left six sons and four daughters. This family was hardly less remarkable than Ruth's, but we must content ourselves with only a rapid survey of their history. We shall not in this connection attempt to trace the descendants of the four daughters. The following is the significant epitaph on Eldad Taylor's tomb-stone in Westfield, Mass. :

"Kind reader, this stone informs you *who* we were. *What* we were, we tell you not. What we *ought* to have been, that be thou. Where we are now you will know hereafter. Remember that 'Christ is the Resurrection and the Life.'"

The six sons were Eldad, Edward, James, Samuel, Jedediah, and John. Four of these were at different times members of the State Legislature, three of Massachusetts, and the youngest of Connecticut.

Eldad, the eldest of the six, was one of the first wife's children, but, losing his mother at the age of four, he came early under the care of Thankful Taylor. One of his descendants is Dr. Charles Fayette Taylor, the manager of the establishment for curing curvatures of the spine, etc., on 53d Street, New-York. He has numerous other descendants scattered through northern New-York and the Eastern States.

Edward. the eldest son of Thankful, has also a large posterity. He left several children, "all of whom were decidedly religious," and some have given liberally to charitable purposes. His daughter, Mary, married Rev. Jonathan Nash, and was the mother of Rev. Ansel Nash. Roland Mather, of Hartford, a corporate member of the A.B.C.F.M., was another descendant; as was the wife of John B. Eldridge, another of the first members of this Missionary Band. The Morgan Brothers, Homer and Henry T., of New-York, are connected with the Taylors, through Pamelia, another daughter of Edward. Thus we find the links connecting ministerial circles, mission bands, and business firms. Turning to Hon. James Taylor's family, we are made acquainted with a son, Rev. James Taylor, of Sunderland, Massachusetts, and among his descendants are Rev. James F. Taylor, of Michigan, and Rev. James Taylor Dickinson, of Connecticut, one of our foreign missionaries to the East.

We must pass by others,—there is much to be yet learned by investigating the history of this large family,— and devote our brief remaining space to Rev. John Taylor, of Deerfield, Massachusetts. He, like his father, was the fourteenth child of the Westfield home. His brother Eldad had been married eight years before John was born. Bereft during his boyhood years of his father, he must have owed much to his mother. How much the world owes her they never will know. Thankful Taylor did her work faithfully. She survived her husband twenty-six years. Her children, even to the youngest, were thoroughly fitted for their work. John, a graduate of Yale, was the family offering to the priesthood. He served at one time in the Connecticut Legislature, but he was best known for his work in the ministry. For nineteen years he was the pastor of the Congregational Church in Deerfield. He married "a child of the Mayflower," a descendant of Governor Bradford, and was the father of eleven children, seven of whom—five sons and two daughters—lived to years of maturity. His eldest daughter, Elizabeth, married her cousin, Rev. James Taylor, of Sunderland, Mass. She and her husband died within a week of each other, leaving nine children, the eldest scarcely of age and the youngest not six months old; yet these children of many prayers all lived to honor their family. One of the sons rose to the head of the greatest mercantile company in Charleston, S. C., and one of the daughters, Julia Taylor, married Rev. Mr. Hyde, through whose family the influence of good parentage may be traced still on. Harriet, the other daughter, married Mr. Roderick Terry. of Hartford, and left at her death eight children. In this family we are introduced to Rev. Roderick Terry, D. D.,* of Peekskill. N. Y., her grandson.

Of the five sons of Rev. John Taylor, three have been deacons in the Congregational Church, and a son of the youngest, Frank D. Taylor, of Detroit, Mich., has been President of the Young Men's Christian Association of the United States.

But the best-known of all Rev. John Taylor's five sons is Hon. Henry Wyllys Taylor, of Canandaigua, N. Y., late Judge of the Supreme Court of this State. We

---

* At the present publication of this article, he is Pastor of the South Reformed Church, New-York.

are indebted to him for a large amount of the knowledge we have of this remarkable mother and her descendants. Judge Taylor being her nearest living relative, only removed two generations from Ruth's own nursery, has treasured up much of the family story.

Although these sketches, as given by us, have been imperfect, we are sure that every one who delights to note the fulfilment of God's promises to the faithful must be interested in the harvest of Ruth, whose descendants in the ministry may be reckoned by nearly half a hundred, who has representatives in the wide mission-fields of the East and of the West, among the mountains of Asia and in the isles of the sea, whose sons have molded our institutions of learning, and whose law-makers have been exalted to almost every position of trust in our nation. Is not the record of such a family worth preserving?

The sheaves of Ruth can never be fully numbered here, but we trust that the story will yet be more complete, and that many more of the faithful laborers of her family will yet "be known in the gates" of the world's wide field.

www.ingramcontent.com/pod-product-compliance
Lightning Source LLC
Chambersburg PA
CBHW032357020726
47499CB00008B/2788